SHORT STORIES
By
ALICE McNEISH

SHORT STORIES by ALICE McNEISH

Edited by George McNeish with help from other family members.

©2018

Artwork by Ed de Jong
© 2018 by Ed de Jong
dejonged@gmail.com
Used by permission

Layout and Graphic Design by George McNeish

Photographs from family archives

Special thanks to Evelyn Gould,
Kerry Leblanc-Gould
& Ed de Jong.
Your contributions, advice and expertise helped make this book possible.

ISBN-13: 978-1986515986
ISBN-10: 1986515982

Published by George McNeish
www.9li.ca

Sowing Peace initiative
www.sowingpeace.ca

Preface

Alice McNeish, my mother, had a dream. I did not know about it. During my youth I would sometimes talk to her about what I hoped to accomplish and I remember her telling me that, although it is nice to dream, we need to be more practical when planning our future. When I read "A DORMANT DREAM" I finally realized what she was talking about.

Her dream was frustrated throughout her life. It struggled to raise its head from time to time and is only now being realized. As an author I felt her frustration. I was motivated to make her dream a reality.

My mom, now entering her 90th year, cannot even remember writing these stories when she was 57. I did not know about them until recently. Now I anticipate seeing my mother holding a copy of this book in her hands.

My mother's wisdom has guided me through many difficult times, yet there was a whole other side of her that I did not know until I read these stories. Not only were they entertaining but each one contained a valuable lesson. I am now privileged to share this wisdom with others.

"SCHOOL DAZE IN 1943" is her own personal story about entering high school. Although I had experienced summer vacations without modern conveniences, I never gave much thought about how one would live year round without them. This story was an eye opener for me. I believe anyone interested in this period of history, as experienced on a personal level, would love this story.

The three fictional stories give a glimpse into the mind and imagination of my mother. In "GRAMMA CAN'T SAY 'NO'" we are immersed into a turbulent family situation. The main character is filled with self-doubt as she makes decisions that may end up causing her to lose her family.

Our family has been known to be very frugal. Carrying this to an extreme she brought us "MISER'S HOLIDAY." I am not sure if she based any of her characters on actual people but we may all see a little of ourselves in one or more of her characters.

"NEVER TOO OLD" may come across as being a mature woman's fantasy, but similarities between the story and her situation at the time could leave one wondering.

My mother's stories are educational and entertaining. She is a great author. I will do my best to follow in her footsteps. It is more than my hope, but my belief that you will thoroughly enjoy these following pages.

CONTENTS

A DORMANT DREAM

A DORMANT DREAM

Through the years my dream of becoming a writer was continually squashed. During my public school days I lived on a backwoods farm where it was difficult to either read or write. Books were scarce at home and at school, but I tried to read everything I could get my hands on. At that time it was considered extravagant to waste paper, so my writing would be squeezed into unusual places. I would use the back of old notebooks, left-over wallpaper, and sometimes precious writing paper. On the farm, reading was ranked with laziness during the daylight hours when there was work to do. We didn't have electricity, so at night, reading or writing by lamplight wasted kerosene.

My parents were conservative and thought it was unnecessary for a farm girl to be "schooled", but my public school teacher encouraged me to continue my education. Due to the shortage of help during the war, farm children were excused from attending school at the age of fourteen. However, my dream of writing would not leave me, so I begged to go to High School.

My five years of secondary school were disappointing because English was the only subject I had trouble with. Each year I failed the first two examinations, but somehow managed to scrape through on the final. Why was English my worst subject?

First of all, a good English student had to be a good speller. I wasn't. Even yet an instant spelling dictionary is at my right hand as I write.

Secondly, a good student had to be long-winded and fill up space on an English exam. I made my point quickly with the least number of words and my script was small.

Thirdly, I couldn't think like the teacher. I soon learned that my opinion wasn't worth much, even though the question clearly asked for it.

Fourthly, there were all sorts of rules and regulations for sentence structure. Long clumsy words and expositions were encouraged.

With these restrictions I could not express myself. By the time I finished secondary school, my dream of becoming a writer was mutilated.

Lack of money halted my formal education and I became a "stay at home" mother of nine. Family life kept me busy, but I often relaxed with my pen. I wrote when I was sad and when I was glad. I wrote to make decisions and to think clearly. Writing was therapy and helped me to be honest with myself. Through the years the hope of becoming a writer was put aside and the dream lay dormant.

Ten years became twenty. At last the dream stirred and raised its sleepy head. During the summer of 1971 I took an English essay course at a local university and, much to my surprise, the written word had changed. My writing was accepted and even praised. Thus encouraged, I completed a variety of interest courses at various education levels, but something was missing.

I was trying to ignore the dream which had awakened and was gaining strength. Of course, doubt kept nagging. "Are you crazy? Writing! At your age? You know you have no time." These thoughts were added to countless other "reasonable" excuses that demanded consideration.

This time the dream refused to be stifled. Even though I was fifty-seven years old I knew I had to write. Where should I start? After studying many course descriptions from several institutions in the fall of 1986, I enrolled in a correspondence course that matched my needs.

Then the dream became master and the dreamer a willing slave. The dream knew no limit and the dreamer found new strength. Now the dream screams for recognition and the dreamer's excited fingers type rapidly. Inspirations flow. Ideas grow. Words glow. Years open wide. Hidden stories come alive. The dream becomes reality. A writer is born.

School Daze in 1943

School Daze in 1943

Alice McNeish

Preface

This story, which took place in a small Ontario town, is true. Only names of people and places have been changed.

School Daze in 1943

I anxiously awaited the results of my High School entrance examinations and each day, after the mailman came, I ran up the lane to look in the mailbox. It seemed like years before the big envelope arrived. My name was spelled wrong, but I recognized the calligraphic handwriting of my school inspector. I quickly opened the letter. Expecting something like a report card with a list of marks, it took me a few seconds to realize that I was holding my Secondary School Entrance Certificate. I passed! This certificate meant that I could go to High School.

I went flying down the lane, waving my precious certificate. Daddy was haying in the front field with the boys. As he turned around to look at the hay loader dumping hay onto the wagon, he glanced at me and smiled. Even the horses looked my way and nodded their heads as they slowly plodded along in front of the wagon.

I ran around the house to the summer kitchen, where Mother was preparing the noon dinner. She smiled, "So you passed, eh? Good for you. Better hurry and set the table. Daddy and the boys will be in soon."

"Do you think Daddy will let me go to High School?"

"Now don't get any foolish notions. You know we can't afford it."

I remembered Miss Morgan, my last teacher, emphasizing the necessity of continuing one's education. There had to be a way to become the teacher or nurse Miss Morgan talked about. How could this be just a foolish notion?

Rain interrupted the haying that afternoon and the chores got finished early. The routine of milking the cows and feeding the animals was simply called "chores." That night, Daddy had a little time to relax. When I saw him smoking his pipe, sitting in his favourite chair tipped back against the wall, I decided to approach him.

"Daddy, I really want to go to High School."

"Who put that crazy idea into your head?"

"It isn't crazy, Daddy. I know I could be a great teacher or nurse and I'd work hard to become one."

"Now Alice, you know you can't work hard. You're too thin and frail. And what about your eyesight? That's a real problem when you have to study books all the time."

"But Daddy, I read all the time anyway and it doesn't bother me with these new glasses. I might be thin, but you know how hard I can work in the fields.

"Yes, that's true. But we really need you here and you'll just get married later anyway. A farmer's wife doesn't need an education.

"I know I have to stay in town to go to school, but I'll be home on weekends and all summer. That's the time when you need me most. I'll do all I can at home too, really I will."

I could see I was finally getting to him. Daddy liked to appear hard, but was soft as a kitten underneath his tough exterior. Nothing was said for awhile. He continued smoking his pipe, his chair was still tipped back and his head was against the wall. Mother hated this and gave him a disapproving glance. He sat up straight and said to Mother, "Do you think Isabel would let her stay there?" I couldn't believe my ears. I felt like dancing and shouting, but I knew I must quietly listen as my parents made plans for my future.

Mother answered, "Isabel does take in roomers and she might have room for Alice. I think she charges a dollar a week. Alice could take food from home and cook her own meals, but she would have to have a little money to buy things that spoil easily. Isabel would see that she

20

doesn't get into trouble, so she would be safe there."

Isabel was Mother's first cousin. It wasn't proper to call an older person by their first name so I called her "Aunt Belle". She visited us occasionally, but I had never been to her house. In fact I rarely went to town, not even to see a doctor or dentist.

Mother was very worried about getting the right clothes for me to wear at High School. She told me I couldn't go in the hand-me-downs I had worn to Public School. I now had to look and act like a proper lady. Yards of material were purchased and while Mother made my wardrobe, I cooked, baked and scrubbed. At that time I was proud of my new clothes, but later, I realized that I wasn't "in style". Of course, I didn't have the heart to tell Mother.

I was very excited when I arrived at Aunt Belle's the night before school started. Aunt Belle took me upstairs to the room I was sharing with two other girls. There were three beds in the room and I was thankful mine was at the back next to the window. We went back downstairs and Aunt Belle showed me an empty shelf in the pantry off the kitchen, where I could store my food and dishes. In the kitchen there was a big iron range which burned coal and wood where I would be cooking my meals. In hot weather I was supposed to cook on an electric hot plate but at first I was afraid to touch it.

There was no electricity at home and something as simple as electric lights fascinated me. That first night I remember the awesome sight of rows and rows of street lights. The dreamer in me pictured them as strings of giant golden beads lighting the path to my invisible future. In 1943 most farms had electricity, tractors and other modern conveniences, so, for most farm students the adjustment to town life was not as traumatic as mine.

This was the first time I had ever been away from home overnight and the apprehension of a new school and the strangeness of my new surroundings prevented me from sleeping. I got up and sat looking out the window at the dimly lit garden, and waited for morning. As dawn approached, cabbage heads in the garden looked up at me with their funny-face grins, trying to reassure me. At sunrise the orange pumpkins took on a fluorescent glow, sending warmth to my shivering, apprehensive body.

I nearly jumped out of my wits when suddenly the clanging of an alarm clock broke the silence. Elsie stirred in the bed next to mine, reached over and turned it off. It was hard to believe Norma was still fast asleep in the third bed. Elsie looked at me and said, "Excited about school, eh? It's only six o'clock so you better go back to sleep. You're lucky you don't have to get up early and go to work."

Elsie sounded so friendly as she hurried about making her bed. "What do you do?" I asked.

"Work at the basket factory. So, of course, I make baskets. Just look at my hands. That's from bending handles and stapling them to the baskets." Her slender hands were rough and red, almost raw looking. Her fingernails were chipped and broken. "Take it from me kid," she continued, "Stay in school. I dropped out when I was sixteen and I've kicked myself for it ever since. I've got to go." Elsie grabbed her housecoat and headed for the bathroom.

Before Mother went home the previous night, she had said to me, "Isabel would be shocked if she knew you didn't know how to turn on a tap or flush the toilet, so come with me

23

and I'll show you." Everything had seemed so complicated but after Elsie returned I decided to try my luck in the bathroom. At that moment I would have felt more comfortable cleaning up at home in the old washroom pumping the water into the wash basin. Also, running out to the outhouse seemed much easier than worrying about flushing a toilet. As I walked out of the bathroom I was very proud of myself. I had remembered everything, or so I thought. I was back in my room, busy getting dressed, when Aunt Belle yelled, "Who left the tap in the bathroom dripping?"

"I guess it was me, I'm sorry," I apologized.

Aunt Belle's loud demand must have wakened Norma who jumped out of bed, screaming that she was late again. Aunt Belle explained that Norma does this every morning.. "Don't pay no mind to her", she said. "But remember you have to squeeze that tap hard to stop it from dripping. Water, especially hot water, costs a lot of money in town.

"You mean you have to pay for water?"

"Sure do. But we don't have to pump it like you folks." Aunt Belle's concerned blue eyes examined me more closely and she said, "Alice, you look awful pale. Are you alright?"

"Oh yes, Aunt Belle, but I am terrified of going to High School."

"Come along and have a good breakfast. That'll fix you up."

My knotted stomach, however, wouldn't let me take one bite. Aunt Belle followed me outside as I was leaving for school. I turned around and asked, "Tell me again, which way I must go to get to school. I am so afraid of getting lost."

"Alice, the school is only two blocks away. You can't get lost. But, oh look, there's Ida. She'll be in Grade Ten this year. I'll ask her if she will take you with her."

I don't know what I would have done without Ida. We went up the hill, then turned right and there before me was Forestown High School. I was shaking as I climbed the steps. Ida tried to reassure me by saying, "I know how you feel. That's how I felt last year. Now I can't imagine why I was so scared." Ida took me up another flight of steps inside the school and pointed to a door. "Grade Nines go there. By the way, do you want to buy my books? You'll find out today what you need. Let me know."

"Thanks for everything," I said as we parted.

I stepped inside the classroom, which was almost empty. It was a big room with rows and rows of desks, about twice the size of the public school I had attended for eight years. My uncertain eyesight made me choose a front desk in the centre row. As I sat waiting, the room filled and by nine o'clock several students were standing with no more desks available. However, portable desks were dragged in and finally everyone found a seat.

Mr. Sears, the principal and also the math teacher, introduced himself and informed us we had a record breaking class of fifty-one. By Grade Ten, he predicted, only half of us would be there and only one fifth of us would graduate five years later. I fervently hoped to be one of the graduates.

There were five teachers, including the principal. Each teacher gave us a list of textbooks and supplies needed for each subject, and we were given the afternoon off to purchase these items which were available at the drugstore. Mother came to town to buy my books, which were expensive, so Ida's offer of second-hand books was gratefully accepted. At that time nothing was supplied by the school board.

My room was only one block away from Main Street, the commercial part of town. Mother told me to go to the grocery store for milk and the bake shop for bread. There was no refrigerator where I roomed so it was necessary to replace perishable food frequently. Mother gave me one dollar a week to do this.

I had never bought anything in my life before, so I waited as long as I could, postponing the ordeal of going to the store. Once there, I must have looked as terrified as I felt because the clerk said, "Is there anything wrong?"

"I want to buy some milk," I answered.

"What size?"

"I.... don't know." I felt so stupid. I never thought of milk having a size. I added, "The smallest, I guess."

The clerk put a pint of milk on the counter and said, "That'll be five cents." I handed her my precious dollar bill and she gave me the change. Remembering Daddy's warning to count the change I sorted it out in my hands, counting it carefully. By this time, several people were staring at me, so I grabbed the milk and headed across the street for bread. It was much easier in the bake shop because I asked for bread "in the smallest size." I was able to buy a half-size loaf there for five cents. Then I ran home, feeling much safer in my room.

After coming from a small country school with one teacher for all eight grades, it was difficult to adjust to a large classroom and five teachers. At first my shyness made it impossible for me to speak or read in front of the class. The only teacher provoked by this was Mr. Sears, the principal. Math was my best subject and although I knew the answers to his questions, I couldn't get over my stage fright.

During the first term he often humiliated me. Aiming his pointer in my direction, Mr. Sears would demand, "Alice, stand up." I would stand up. "Now answer this question." He would point at the blackboard. His dark piercing eyes scowled at me over gold-rimmed glasses and fifty pairs of eyes stabbed me from the other three sides. To avoid all these eyes, I hung my head and stared at the boards in the wooden floor.

Minutes that seemed like hours, dragged on. The teacher tapped his pointer as he waited for me to answer. My legs turned to rubber and then to jelly. Just in time to save me from collapsing Mr. Sears would yell, "Sit down, you stupid fool! Why are you taking up space in this classroom?" Actually he called me something worse than "a stupid fool," but that can't be repeated here.

One thing Mr. Sears did was make me boiling mad. I smouldered, fumed and raged. I was used to hiding my feelings, so no one knew how I felt. If I complained at home, my chances of staying in school would be ruined. Work was my only outlet. I did my homework diligently. I studied earnestly. I slaved at home willingly. There seemed to be no way of removing the only obstacle in my path, namely Mr. Sears.

Finally, this burden was lifted in a way that surprised both of us. In January we learned the results of our first term examinations and Mr. Sears came into the classroom, loaded down with the math exam papers. He picked the top paper off the pile and laid it on my desk. I saw one hundred percent scrawled across the top. I was very much aware that he continued to stand right beside my desk and I kept staring at the paper on my desk to avoid looking at him. Then I heard him make this astonishing remark, "This is the first completely perfect paper I have ever marked." I should have been flattered and maybe I was. However, it was his next gesture that both shocked and amazed me. He said, "Alice, I am giving you these two War Saving Stamps as a peace offering. I hope someday you will come out of your shell. In the meantime I will not ask you any more questions in class." He kept his promise and I no longer dreaded math class. The proverbial stone was rolled away and I was able to continue my education in peace.

I graduated from Forestown High School five years later. Of course, Daddy was right. I was married a few months after graduating. I did, however, become both a teacher and a nurse in the eyes of my family.

School Daze in 1943

Editor's note: *Alice Horsburgh, later McNeish, went to Mount Forest High School in Mount Forest, Ontario.*

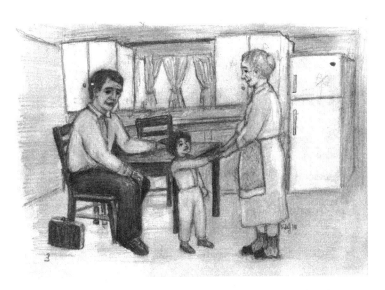

GRAMMA CAN'T SAY "NO"

GRAMMA CAN'T SAY "NO"

Alice McNeish

Melissa would arrive after lunch and Mildred McLacey was happily preparing for the visit of her four year old granddaughter. Although Melissa only lived about twenty kilometers away Mildred did not see her as often as she would have liked. Roger, her son, was always "too busy." Remembering how much Melissa liked playing with play dough, Mildred decided to make some from an old recipe she used when Roger was young.

Her son kept creeping into her thoughts and she had an uneasy feeling that something was bothering him. When she questioned him about it, he would put her off saying, "Oh, Mom, you're always worrying about something." No doubt he was right, but still she could not help wondering. Maybe it was just the added responsibility of the new baby. Little Katie would be two months old now and Mildred could hardly wait to see her. Roger's wife, Debbie, was a wonderful mother for the little girls.

The doorbell interrupted her thoughts and Mildred hurried to receive her visitors. As she opened the door Melissa gleefully jumped into her arms and they hugged and kissed each other several times. "I love you Gramma," Melissa kept repeating with the rambunctious enthusiasm of a four year old. "That's enough, Melissa," Roger reprimanded, "You'll make Gramma too tired to keep you for the weekend and you wouldn't like that, would you?"

"Where's Debbie and the baby?" Mildred asked.

"Deb decided to stay at home. Katie kept her up last night and she was tired. You know how it is with a new baby. I hope you understand. I knew you'd be disappointed if they didn't come, but Deb just wasn't up to it." Roger seemed to be making unnecessary excuses which added to Mildred's uneasiness.

She knew there was no use prying so she accepted his explanation and said, "Well, have a cup of coffee with me before you leave." The cup of coffee turned into a small lunch, with Melissa chattering all the time. Roger finished eating much too quickly. He got up from the table and said, "I really have to get back to work, Mom."

"I wish you wouldn't work so hard, Roger. You need to relax more, and be with your family."

"There you go again, Mom, always worrying." Then, patting Melissa on the head, he added, "I hope this little blabbermouth won't be too much trouble for you."

"Of course not," she assured him while pulling Melissa onto her knee. "Melissa and I are going to have a great time."

Roger smiled as he bent over and kissed them both. "You'll probably spoil her rotten," he remarked as he left.

It didn't take Melissa long to notice the play dough and together they made models of the whole family. The little girl proudly pointed to each one saying, "This is Mommy. This is Daddy. This is Katie. This is me." Then, as if the thought suddenly occurred to her, she looked up at Mildred and asked, "Gramma, why do Mommy and Daddy fight?"

"What did you say?" Mildred hoped she had misunderstood the question.

"Mommy and Daddy really do fight, Gramma."

"Now, dear, you don't mean that. Sometimes big people have disagreements but that's not really fighting."

"But I heard them when I was in bed. Mommy said she wanted to leave Daddy. Does that mean they're getting a div—divorce?"

"Melissa, whatever gave you that idea and who told you about divorce?"

"Adam, my friend. His Daddy doesn't live at his house. My Daddy won't go away, will he?" she asked, tears filling her trusting dark eyes.

"Now, now, Melissa, I'm sure you don't understand. You've been hearing too many crazy stories. Your Mommy and Daddy wouldn't do anything like that. Come along now and we'll make some cookies. Remember the funny shapes we made the last time you were here?"

Melissa's enthusiasm returned and she soon, forgot her troubles. Mildred wished that she could do the same. Hampered by her granddaughter's energetic help, she finally rolled out the cookie dough and she watched as the chubby little hands tried to push the cookie cutter through the dough. Her thoughts kept returning to Roger. Was her intuition, concerning him right? Was that why Debbie stayed home today? Was there a reason for Melissa's fears?

"Help me do this one, Gramma," a little voice broke into her meandering thoughts. Mildred smiled as Melissa handed her the cutter, scrambled off the chair and ran into the family room to turn on the television, the cookies instantly forgotten. She soon was glued to cartoons and Mildred finished baking the cookies with no interruptions.

Grandmother and granddaughter were real pals that weekend as they played games, sang songs, coloured pictures and went for walks. Mildred didn't consider herself old, but trying to keep up with this active youngster thoroughly exhausted her. She was quite relieved when Roger came to pick up his daughter.

Mildred noticed again that Roger came without Debbie and Katie, but Melissa was making such a scene that there was no time for enquiries. The little tyke begged, then demanded to stay. "I don't want my coat on, Daddy I'm staying at Gramma's," she stated, clutching onto her grandmother.

"But, Melissa, don't you want to go home and see Mommy and baby Katie?" Roger asked. There was a moment of indecision, but she still refused to leave. Finally, Roger had to pick her up and carry her to the car, kicking and screaming all the way. Mildred followed them outside and Melissa, realizing she couldn't get her own way, hugged and kissed her grandmother many times before they drove away. Tears fell on the wrinkled cheek as she turned back to the empty house.

Although Mildred lived by herself, she was too busy to be lonely, but there were times when she felt alone and this was one of them. Her concern for Roger deepened. Due to the turmoil of Melissa's parting she didn't get a chance to mention Melissa's story to Roger. She thought he should know about it, even if it wasn't true; and it did seem strange that he came to pick up Melissa by himself. "Oh, well. Guess I can't do much about it," she said to herself, as she turned on the TV and picked up the afghan she was crocheting.

A few days later while she was putting out the garbage, Mildred was surprised to see Roger pulling into the driveway. One look at him told her that something terrible had happened. She put her hand on his shoulder and quickly led him into the house. "I can't believe it," he mumbled, "Tell me it's not true."

"What—what are you talking about?" his mother exclaimed, with racing thoughts conjuring all sorts of horrible things.

"Debbie left me. I came home from work and found a note," Roger blurted. "I can't believe

41

she would actually do it." He was breathing heavily and staring wildly around the room.

Mildred tried to comfort him saying, "It's not the end of the world, Roger. I'm sure she'll come back after she thinks it over. What about the kids?"

"Of course she has them too and that's the worst of it. I'll probably never see them again." He grabbed a picture of Melissa off the television and Mildred thought he was going to tear it up, so she put out her hand to take it from him.

"Oh Roger, don't think like that. Of course you'll see them again. Fathers have a right to see their children even if it comes to divorce."

"I'm not that kind of a father and you haven't heard everything yet." His prominent Adam's apple bobbed up and down as he swallowed several times before continuing. Mildred waited quietly for her son to get hold of himself before he continued.

"You won't believe this, Mom, but Debbie went to Thelma House, the home for battered wives."

"Oh no, Roger. Surely you didn't—"

"No, of course not. What do you think I am? I never touched her and that's the gospel truth, no matter what you might hear."

"But why did she go there?"

"She smacked her eye on the corner of a cupboard door. She's always leaving them open. She really got a shiner. I expect that's what gave her the idea of going to Thelma House."

"But surely they wouldn't believe her."

"You don't know Deb. She can really pour on the sob stuff when she wants to. I could even be charged with assault and battery."

"Don't say such a thing. I'm sure Debbie wouldn't go that far."

"I don't know and I don't care. She's ruined me. Six years gone down the drain just like that."

"Roger, dear," Mildred soothed, "Please don't give up so quickly. Things often look worse than they really are. Maybe there's something I can do to help."

"Mom, I'm telling you right now, keep out of this. You can't help and neither can anyone else.

I didn't come here for help. I just wanted to tell you what happened before someone else did."

"Debbie and I always got along, so maybe she will still let the children visit me and you could see them here."

"No, mom, no! You don't understand. I can't be just a weekend father. For me it's all or nothing. If Debbie and the children don't come home where they belong, I never want to see any of them again."

Yes, thought Mildred, Roger was always like that. All through school this thin, dark-headed boy worked hard to get top marks, and later he slaved at his job with Better Foods until he became District Manager. The fragile old lady heaved a sigh of exasperation as she realized that the stubborn determination that made him so successful in business was the very thing that was ruining his marriage.

"I've got to get back to the office," Roger continued, "though I don't know why."

Mildred watched as Roger's new compact car pulled away into the street. She hated to see her son so unhappy. Twisting her apron with nervous hands she walked from room to room.

Noticing the picture face down on the television, she picked it up and stared at Melissa's mischievous smile. The thought of losing her grandchild was too much for her and she collapsed into a nearby armchair and wept.

She barely remembered the next few days. Every time she phoned Roger at home there was no answer. She was afraid to phone him at work so she suffered alone. In almost every room of her rambling bungalow there had been pictures of the grandchildren which reminded her of the painful situation. Now, they were all packed away in a box along with toys and knick-knacks. She felt guilty about packing them away, but the pain she felt every time she saw them was too much. She still hoped Roger and Debbie would get back together. Roger was her only child and his girls her only grandchildren.

The phone was ringing. Her heart beat wildly as she answered it. "Hi, Gramma. "She was shocked to hear Debbie's voice. "I know you didn't expect to hear from me."

At first, Mildred couldn't find words to reply, then she stammered, "No... no, I guess I didn't. Is everything all right?"

"If you mean, 'Are Roger and I back together again?' then the answer is 'No.'"

"Oh."

"The reason I called is that I'm having trouble with Melissa. She wakes up screaming at night and mopes around all day. I thought you might be able to help. That is if you want to."

Mildred felt like a traitor when she answered, "Yes, yes, of course. Can you bring her here?"

"I could be there in half an hour. Would that be alright?"

"I'll be looking for you." Mildred replaced the receiver on the phone and sighed. She felt relieved to hear from Debbie. She had always liked the girl and they had grown closer after the children arrived. Debbie had started calling her "Gramma" in a loving respectful way.

She suddenly remembered that Roger had told her not to interfere, but, what could she do? Debbie sounded as if she really needed her and her concern for the grandchildren was stronger than Roger's warning.

As promised Debbie and the children arrived a half hour later. Melissa squealed with delight as she ran into her grandmother's waiting arms.

Everything seemed so normal as Mildred waited for Debbie to free the baby from the car seat and carry her into the house. Little Katie was sleeping, so Mildred turned the armchair against the wall and the chubby little infant was laid in the makeshift crib. Melissa was tugging on her dress so Mildred picked her up and hugged her again.

The women stood silently looking at each other then Mildred motioned for them to be seated. Debbie's straight blond hair bounced as she turned to her mother-in-law. Her freckled face made her look young and innocent although the fading purple mark under her eye couldn't be concealed with makeup.

"I'm sorry for coming here like this," she began, "but I didn't know what else to do." Mildred didn't know what to say, so she waited for her to continue. "I couldn't stand it anymore, Gramma. All Roger can think of is work, work, work. I may as well be a widow. Melissa sees so little of her father she keeps asking if he has gone away like Adam's father. I tried to arrange for him to spend more time with her saying that the new baby was tiring me out. I asked him to look after her for one weekend. But what did he do? He dumped her on you just so he could go back to his precious work."

"Debbie, don't say 'dumped.' I was more than happy to have her. Surely you know that."

"I'm sorry. Guess I got carried away. I shouldn't be here criticizing your son. Please forgive me."

"Don't worry about it, Debbie. I'm glad you brought the children here. Roger told me you went to Thelma House."

"It's not what you think, Gramma. Roger never beat me or anything like that. I went to Thelma House several times before I made the decision to leave. They were so understanding and I needed someone to talk to. As you know all my relatives live so far away. I know Roger thought it was because of the black eye and I didn't make him any the wiser. All we seem to do lately is argue. I finally decided it would be better if we separated. I didn't have anywhere else to go."

"Melissa told me you were fighting. It's none of my business, but surely you must realize that Roger is just trying to get ahead. You have a lovely home and I don't think money is a problem."

"That's true, Gramma. But money isn't everything. I didn't marry money; I married Roger, a caring and loving man. Now he has become a machine only interested in work. Since he became District Manager we hardly see each other. I can't exist with that kind of relationship."

"Well, Debbie, I don't know what to say. Have you tried marriage counselling?"

"Are you kidding? Roger wouldn't hear of it and, to tell the truth, I think it would be a waste of time."

"I see."

"I tried phoning Roger, but he won't even discuss anything unless I come crawling back to him. I belong there, he says, like one of his possessions." Melissa was looking for something to play with, but the bitterness in her mother's voice made her turn around and look at Debbie who quickly changed the subject. "Gramma, the real reason I came here was to ask if you could keep the children for a little while. I can stay with a friend until I find a job and an apartment, but the children would be a lot happier here. Melissa made an awful fuss at the home. I know I'm asking a lot from you and I'll understand if you say 'No.'" Debbie waited for Mildred's answer.

The grandmother was torn in two. Roger told her not to interfere. One look at Melissa's face told her that her granddaughter needed her. She also knew that Debbie didn't have anywhere else to take them. So, what else could she do?

"You know the children are always welcome here. I just wish that you and Roger could sort things out. I hope you find an apartment soon. Roger would blow his top if he knew I had the children."

Melissa was happy with her grandmother but she kept asking when her parents were coming to pick her up. Little Katie was learning to smile and occasionally Mildred would be rewarded with a flickering grin. Caring for the children would have been a real pleasure but she felt so guilty knowing that Roger would not approve. At times she thought she should phone Debbie and tell her she could no longer keep the children. She even thought of phoning Roger and confessing what she had done. However, yesterday floated into tomorrow and the little girls stayed with their grandmother. Mildred's guilt put her on edge and she kept hearing cars pull into her driveway. She would jump up to look out the window fearing that she would see Roger's little brown car pulling into the driveway.

One afternoon the children were asleep and Mildred made use of this time to catch up with laundry. The washer and dryer were running and she didn't hear Roger until he was standing in the doorway. With evidence of children all through the house, there was no doubt that he knew that the children were there. Mildred waited for the blast.

"Why, Mom, why?"

"I couldn't help it Roger. I love them. They're my grandchildren, my only grandchildren." Tears fell on the wet clothes as she pleaded with her raging son.

"I told you not to interfere," he screamed at her. "I can't believe you would actually do this. I wouldn't be surprised if Deb is here too. I'll bet you put her up to phoning me about marriage counselling."

"Cool down, Roger, and let me explain. When Debbie asked me to keep the children I just couldn't say 'No.'" Mildred put her hand on her son's shoulder but he flung it aside angrily.

"Cool down, eh?" he started pacing back and forth. "I'm telling you right now to get them out of this house or you will never. …"

Suddenly Melissa ran into the room squealing with delight, "Daddy, Daddy, I knew you'd come." She raised her arms for him to pick her up. Mildred held her breath. The dryer had stopped. The room was silent. Time stood still. All of them were motionless, unable to think, unable to act. Roger stared at the little arms still raised to him. A soft questioning "Daddy, can we go home now?" brought them all back to life. Roger picked up his little daughter who wrapped her arms tightly around his neck. Mildred escaped to look after the baby who had started crying.

She picked up Katie from the makeshift nursery and hugged her closely. Weakness caused her to sink into the nearby rocking chair. The baby stopped crying but Mildred sobbed her heart out as she rocked to and fro. This may be the last time she would hold her grandchild. She did not see Roger come into the room, carrying Melissa. His hand on her shoulder startled her.

"Why are you crying, Gramma?" Melissa asked.

It was Roger who answered. "Gramma's crying because Daddy's been bad." Still holding Melissa, he put his free arm around his mother and the baby. Katie looked up at him and gave him one of her rare, precious smiles.

Softly Roger murmured, as if talking to himself, "I didn't know she could smile." Mildred stopped weeping but remained silent. She was afraid of breaking the spell; afraid that at any minute Roger's anger might return. Even Melissa sensed the tension and hugged her Daddy more tightly.

Finally, Roger spoke, more tenderly than she had ever heard him speak "Mom, I glad you couldn't say 'No.' I've been a pig headed fool to think I could survive without my family. — Mom, I've been through hell this past two weeks. My job just doesn't seem so important anymore."

"Daddy, are we going home now?" Melissa looked straight into her father's eyes.

Roger could not help but stare back at his little girl. "Family," he said. "Family is what's important."

He paused, but still no one spoke, then he continued. "Never did have much faith in any kind of counselling, but I guess it can't hurt to try. Do you have Deb's phone number?"

MISER'S HOLIDAY

MISER'S HOLIDAY

Alice McNeish

Harry Hackbury returned to his modest bungalow in the outskirts of a progressive Saskatchewan town. Parking his car in the garage, he unlocked the door which opened into his kitchen. He plugged in the kettle to make a pot of tea, which he usually sipped while reading the evening newspaper. But this hot August night he stared at the paper without reading it. Finally he tossed it aside and sat pondering Doctor Erb's advice.

"Harry, you're run down and worn out. You'd better look after yourself before it's too late," the good doctor had warned.

"Just give me something to keep me on my feet." Harry requested.

"That's not the answer," Doctor Erb admonished. "You need a complete rest."

Harry's tea became cold as he absently gazed out the window. How could an undertaker take a holiday? His assistant, Ron Anderson, certainly couldn't take over. After spending years working hard and saving every cent, he now owned the only funeral home in the district and wanted to keep it that way. Some clients grumbled about his high prices and Ron often told him he should be more understanding, but Harry made it plain to Ron that he was running a business, not a charity.

The heat was becoming unbearable, so Harry rose to open the front window in the living room. As he passed the mirrored wall he stopped and looked at his reflection. He patted his perfectly groomed hair which was parted in the middle. At fifty-three there was no sign of baldness and he thought the slight greying at the temple added dignity to his appearance. Under closer scrutiny he noticed dark, sunken eyes in a pale, thin face. He felt the sharp ridge along his slightly hooked nose and mumbled, "What a scrawny old man you are!"

Then Doctor Erb's voice came back to him again. "I know it's difficult to eat right when you are living alone. Maybe you should consider hiring a cook or eat out at a good restaurant as often as possible." However, Harry had practised thriftiness for so long that hiring domestic help or eating out was unthinkable.

Suddenly, the ringing telephone interrupted his thoughts. "Hackbury Funeral Home," he answered automatically.

"How are you, Harry?" At first he didn't recognize the female voice.

"Who is this?"

"It's your long lost cousin from Regina."

"Oh! Sheila, why are you calling?"

"I was talking to Mom on the phone and she asked me to call you. She says she often thinks of you and wonders how you're doing.

"Is she still away out in B.C.?"

"She's still there, so why don't you give her a call or, better yet, go and see her. You've never been out there, have you?"

"Can't get away" Harry answered abruptly.

"That's too bad. A holiday would be good for you. Are you sure you're alright. You sound kind of weak."

"Probably the phone connection. Anyway, I must go. Say 'Hello' to your Mom for me. Good-bye, Sheila." Harry hated phone conversations, especially long distance calls. Ridiculous how young people wasted money.

Sheila's mother, Aunt Hilda, was his mother's youngest sister. Harry remembered how his mother hated Joe LeVere for eloping with her younger sister when she was only eighteen. For years Uncle Joe wandered from job to job, but now they seemed to be settled near some Indian village in Northern British Columbia. Sheila didn't mention her father and he wondered if Uncle Joe was still living. "Oh well, who cares!" he grumbled, as he drank his cold tea.

The next day Harry went to the funeral home as usual. Ron Anderson came in with some papers which he laid on Harry's desk. Lately he avoided his boss as much as possible because he was becoming so ornery that it was impossible to reason with him. But this time Harry looked so ill that Ron asked, "Are you OK? You look terrible."

"Just a little tired, that's all."

"Why don't you go home and rest, I can take care of things here."

"Maybe I should go home. Are you sure you can manage?"

"Positive. And while we're on the subject, Harry, why don't you take some time off. I've been here for over five years and can easily handle the work during the slow season. You haven't looked a bit well lately. It seems you need a vacation."

"You know I can't do that. See you tomorrow. Don't hesitate to call me if you need anything."

Totally exhausted, Harry arrived home and slept the rest of the day. At last he roused himself and thought, "This can't go on. I've got to do something." Everyone seemed to notice his condition. The doctor advised him to take a holiday. Sheila suggested he visit Aunt Hilda. Even Ron was pressuring him to take some time off. Although he hated to admit it, they were probably right. Ron had enough experience and could handle things for a couple of weeks during the slow summer months. Although he liked to think his business could not operate without him, there really was no reason he couldn't take some time off.

Harry began to formulate a plan. He had worked far too hard to amass his small fortune, so to blow it on a cruise would not do. Vacations cost money and miserly Harry did not spend money on anything that was not absolutely necessary. But to spend a couple of weeks with a relative would not cost much. Sheila had said that Aunt Hilda wanted to see him and he could easily drive himself to B.C. Fresh cool mountain air would be a relief from the summer heat on the prairie. So, yes he would go and visit Aunt Hilda, and to show he was not too cheap he would find some inexpensive little trinket to give her as a thank you gift. That would be a lot cheaper than staying at a tourist resort.

Harry waited until after midnight to take advantage of the lower phone rates before he called Sheila with his news. He got her out of bed and, of course, she was very surprised to hear from him. After quickly telling her his plans, he asked for instructions on how to find her mother's house. Sheila told him exactly how to get to the remote area in northern British Columbia.

"If you have trouble finding it, just ask in the village. Mom still does mission work there and everyone knows her. In fact, she has a lovely native girl living with her. Pauline's only fifteen, but she's a big help to Mom. She'll be thrilled to see you, Harry. You have…"

Sheila was talking too long, so Harry interrupted, "I guess you can phone your mother for me to let her know I'll be going to see her."

"Oh sure. No problem. When can you get away?"

"I'll try to leave a week from Monday, if that's alright with your mother. Let me know if it isn't."

Harry didn't want to make expensive long distance calls and Sheila didn't care about spending money anyway. Anxious to end the conversation, he thanked her and quickly hung up. Then he remembered that he was going to ask about Uncle Joe. Sheila never mentioned him and he wondered again if he was still living. When Sheila phoned back a couple of days later to confirm the arrangement, he was again to anxious to get off the phone to inquire about Uncle Joe.

After much preparation and many last minute instructions for his assistant, he left home in late August. His new compact car was economical on fuel. To save motel expenses he started very early Monday morning expecting to make the trip in two days. However, due to his weakened condition, he had to rest frequently and ended with the expense of having to spend three nights in motels.

On the latter part of his journey, he drove many miles on dangerous logging truck roads. At last he arrived at the Indian village Sheila had mentioned. Then he drove west until he came to a wooden sign, inscribed with the words, "LeVere's Retreat." Assured that he was at the right place, he turned into a dark lane. Trees on each side of the narrow road made

Harry feel like he was driving through a winding tunnel. After climbing higher and higher he suddenly came to a clear flat spot where the lane ended in a circle in front of a strange looking house. As he parked the car, he saw it was a long log cabin built against a hill. This small plateau was completely surrounded by trees and mountains. No morning or evening sunlight would ever touch this place.

"Why on earth would Aunt Hilda live in this isolated God-forsaken place?" Harry asked himself. There was no sign of a living soul and he wondered if the house was deserted. He went up to the front door and lifted the heavy brass door knocker. In the stillness the echo of the sharp clang resounded through the timberland. At first no one responded, but as he was about to return to his car the door quickly opened revealing a slim, dark-haired girl, dressed in a crisp white blouse and a blue denim skirt.

"May I help you?" the young lady asked in a low husky voice.

"Is this LeVere's," Harry asked, noticing how her dark inquisitive eyes studied him from head to toe.

"That's right," she answered cautiously."

"I've… I've come to visit my aunt," Harry announced hesitantly. The thorough inspection was making him nervous.

"You must be Harry Hackbury?"

"Yes. I believe my Aunt Hilda is expecting me."

"Please come in." she said coldly but politely. "Your aunt told me you would be coming."

"Is she home?" he asked, not sure that he should accept the invitation. This young native girl did not seem very trusting of him.

"No. She's over at the village, but she'll be here soon."

Harry guessed she referred to the Indian village he had just come through. Aunt Hilda must still be doing her "good works" with those stupid people. He suddenly became aware that the young lady was still watching him. It was as though she could see through him and read his thoughts. He was sure she despised him as much as he despised those of her race. "I'll wait in the car," he stated abruptly to break the tension.

"Oh no, Mr. Hackbury. Do come in. I'm Pauline and I live here with your aunt. She asked me to look after you if you came when she was away. Please come in." Harry stepped inside and felt even more uncomfortable, "We sort of expected you yesterday," she continued politely, trying to hide her animosity. She didn't want to disappoint Hilda by being rude to this guest, but something in his manners told her he was up to no good.

"Do sit down Mr. Hackbury. Would you like some tea?"

"That would be nice." Harry couldn't understand why this young native seemed so threatening to him. It should be the other way around. She was just a child and very likely his aunt's maid. Harry suddenly felt foolish and put on an air of authority as he commanded. "Yes Miss, bring me some tea."

Pauline's darting eyes quickly x-rayed him again. His aloofness pierced her like an arrow. She had a strong sense that this man did not like her. He likely hated all members of her race and she could not see why his aunt would want him there. Hilda was like a mother to her and this man was her nephew, but surely his presence would come to no good. She started to think of ways to get him to leave.

Harry could feel her stare burning through him. He had heard of the mystic power these savages had and was sure she was reading his thoughts. He avoided eye contact with her out of fear she would read his black soul. Perhaps his idea of taking advantage of a relative he barely knew in order to enjoy a cheap vacation was not as wise as he thought. He knew she worked with these strange people and perhaps had adopted some of their ways. He was not sure what they may do to him if they found out his real reason for this visit.

There was relief when Pauline quietly disappeared into the kitchen. Her moccasins made no noise on the polished wooden floor and Harry feared she may return as quietly as she left and catch him unawares. He distracted himself by looking around the room. The old mismatched furniture looked like it had come from thrift shops. He recognized an oval cherry table that had been in the family for generations, but its legs had been shortened to turn it into a coffee table. That table should have been his. How did Aunt Hilda get possession of this priceless heirloom? It was a disgrace how it had been defiled with the saw.

Then he noticed a smoker's stand beside a black leather arm chair. Was Uncle Joe still alive? Crossing the room for a closer look, he noticed that there were no ashes in the polished stainless steel tray, but a shiny brown pipe rested on the side of the stand. "It appears that Uncle Joe is still living," he surmised although the apparent disuse caused some doubt.

Just then Pauline walked in with a tea tray. Without a word she placed it on the coffee table, waiting quietly as Harry ate the delicious little lemon cakes and sipped the hot reviving tea. Her silent presence made him nervous, so to avoid her discerning gaze he continued to look around the room. His eye kept coming back to the smoker's stand. He had his back to his young hostess when he casually asked, "Is Uncle Joe still around?"

Pauline was trying to be gracious to her friend's nephew, but his rude conduct was infuriating. His question revealed that he did not know the family. Why was he here? He surely had no love for his aunt. She began to test him.

"Didn't you know?" Pauline could see his nervousness as he turned toward her to set his tea cup on the table. "Your Uncle Joe has been gone for a while now, and it is strange that you asked because it was one year ago today that he walked out that door."

Harry noticed that she said gone. She didn't say he died. Perhaps his aunt had finally kicked out that no account deadbeat. But what did she mean by "gone." Maybe he was dead. Harry was getting frustrated with this little game Pauline was playing. What was she up to? Harry was very uncomfortable, but he had to learn more. "What happened?" he asked.

A sad forlorn voice answered him. "See that path through those trees?" Harry turned to see where she was pointing and was surprised to see tears in her dark eyes. She stared into the forest and continued, "He was going hunting and he went that way." After a pause she commented, "I'm surprised you haven't heard about it."

"I don't bother with family very much," he tried to explain. He couldn't understand why Sheila hadn't told him although he didn't care. It seemed no one else cared either. "Someone must have gone looking for him." He stated absentmindedly.

"The whole village searched the countryside for days. They even had a helicopter out looking. My cousin found his nylon hunting bag on top of quicksand. His old green felt hat was also in the area but it was impossible to find the body."

"Indians probably murdered him," Harry thought, and immediately wished he hadn't. He still was not sure if this girl could read his thoughts. "Why does she make me feel like this? It must be my weakened condition." Harry tried to make his tortured mind rest as he heard Pauline's low, soft mesmerizing voice.

"He used to tease me by singing," the young maiden seemed to be talking to herself. Then she softly sang, "There was a sweet little Indian maid, a pretty little mountain maid. Who…." The melodious voice suddenly cracked and Harry notice huge tears rolling down her cheeks. She stared past him out into the forest and added, "Sometimes I still think I hear him in the woods, singing that crazy song."

"I'm sorry," Harry mumbled feigning concern.

Wiping away the tears with the back of her hand, she quickly warned, "Don't say anything to your aunt. She pretends he's still alive. She still gets his meals as if he was living, even sets the table for him. She used to hate his smoking, but now she polishes his smoker's stand and puts the pipe on the side ready for him."

How awful! How could he stay here under these conditions? Feeling very tired and weak, Harry decided to go back to the closest town and find a room. Then he heard the rattle of an engine. He turned and saw an old beat-up station wagon stopping in front of the house.

"There's your Aunt Hilda," Pauline said and ran to open the door for her. A petite, white-haired lady, loaded with parcels, came in. It was more than thirty years since Harry had seen her and he didn't know what to expect. She set the parcels on the floor and rushed over to him. He thought she was going to throw her arms around him and maybe even kiss him. How revolting! Sensing his coldness, she suddenly stopped and politely reached out to shake his hand. "Nice to see you, Harry."

"Nice to see you too, Aunt Hilda," he spoke with stiff formality.

"I'm sorry I wasn't here when you arrived. Did Pauline look after you?"

"Yes, thank you. Your maid gave me some tea."

"Oh, but Pauline's not my maid. She's been part of our family since her parents were killed in a car accident three years ago." Aunt Hilda put her arm around the girl and patted her long black hair "We better hurry and get supper. Uncle Joe will be home soon, hungry as a bear," she said as she picked up her parcels and headed for the kitchen. Pauline glanced over her shoulder at Harry with a "see what I mean" look and he nodded to let her know that he understood.

"Harry, bring in, your belongings and make yourself at home," Aunt Hilda called to him. "I hope you'll feel more comfortable when Joe gets home. I can see you're a little nervous with us women folk."

Harry looked sharply at his aunt. Pauline was standing behind her, sadly shaking her head. "She won't let herself believe he's dead," he thought. "This is terrible. She must be crazy. She should see a psychiatrist. I should leave right away." He considered his options but didn't want to appear rude. He figured he could endure this craziness for one night and that would save him the cost of renting a room.

He felt relief as he stepped out into the crisp cool air. He took his time being in no hurry to re-enter that madhouse. He opened the trunk of his car and looked at his luggage for a moment, taking his time to decide what to pick up first. During that moment of silence, he heard something in the distance. He kept perfectly still and listened quietly. Someone was singing and the tune sounded familiar. It was a man's voice and he began to recognize the words. "There was a sweet little Indian maid, a pretty little mountain maid."

Pauline had said she sometimes heard Uncle Joe singing in the woods. Harry had worked with dead bodies for his entire adult life. It never bothered him to prepare the dead for burial, and he was good at his job. But never in his career had one of his clients come back to life.

The adrenaline pumping through his body caused him to move faster than he had been able to for many years. He slammed the truck lid loudly, jumped into the car, slamming the door as the motor roared to life. Suddenly he was careening down the lane barely keeping on the narrow winding road.

Aunt Hilda had heard the roar of the car engine and raced out of the house to see what was happening. Pauline followed as they watched the car disappear between the trees. While they watched, a man came out of the forest carrying some game and his hunting rifle. He became alarmed thinking the fleeing car was an intruder.

"What's going on here?" he asked.

"I don't know what happened, Joe," Hilda answered bewildered. "That was our nephew that was supposed to be staying with us for a couple of weeks. I don't know why he took off like that.

"Maybe he'll be back," Joe said brightly, then added, "What's for supper?"

At the supper table, Hilda worried about Harry. "Such a strange man," she told Joe. "He seemed so nervous. I thought he might be more relaxed when you came home." Then she turned to Pauline and said, "You talked to him before I got home. Did you know of anything that would cause him to leave so fast?"

Pauline sat thinking for a minute scratching her head. "When he first came to the door, he kept looking around at the long grass, all nervous like. Then he asked me if there were snakes around here. I told him our snakes were harmless. But he still looked terrified."

Joe interrupted, and put into words what the three of them were thinking. "If he's that afraid of nature, I'm glad he left. I can't understand why he wanted to come here so suddenly, after all these years. I hope you're not too disappointed, Hilda?"

"Well no. I remembered him as a young boy and wanted to see him again, but he seemed really out of place here. I'm sort of relieved he's gone."

"Pauline got up from the table and went over and hugged Hilda. Then she sat on Joe's knee and gave him a kiss. "I love you both and would do anything to keep you happy." This time she was telling the truth.

NEVER Too OLD

NEVER Too OLD

Alice McNeish

The first time Edith Elgart remembered seeing this letter carrier was last spring. She was transplanting petunias in the front flower bed and he startled her with a friendly, "Hello." They chatted a couple of minutes. Then she held up her hands to show him they were too dirty to take the mail, so he dropped it in the mailbox and continued on his way.

Edith and her husband were retired and their latest project was converting an old city bus into a motor home. It was parked in their driveway and one beautiful spring day Edith was busy painting the newly installed kitchen cupboards. Her friendly mailman — she never did know his name—poked his head in the door and asked, "What's going on in here?"

"Come in and take a look if you're interested."

He looked all though the bus admiring the makeshift motor home. Then, without invitation, this young man plopped himself on a bench and sat at the kitchen table. "Sure is hot today, he remarked. It seemed unmannerly to continue painting, so Edith reluctantly laid her paintbrush on the pail and sat at the other side of the table.

As he talked she noticed a strange faraway look in his large round eyes. His dark complexion gave him a youthful appearance, but she guessed he would be about thirty years old. As he talked she realized his perpetual smile was only an illusion. His "happy face" appearance was created by a very wide mouth, which spread from ear to ear when he actually did smile.

"I just bought an older home on Water Street," he said.

"Do you like it?"

"Not now. But I'm going to fix it up exactly as I want it."

"What about your wife?"

"I'm divorced and I intended to stay that way." For a second his thin bottom lip quivered with anger, but he quickly switched to a smile and added, "I'd love to fix up something like this."

Edith noticed her paintbrush was beginning to dry out so she went back to her painting. He finally took the hint and left.

Several times he rang her door bell and asked to borrow a pen, explaining that he had to get a signature for registered mail up the street. Edith was a little puzzled by this, wondering why he didn't carry a pen or why he didn't just ask the signer. Although she told him to keep the pen, he always insisted on returning it.

That summer, due to unusual circumstances mail was being delivered to Elgart's address for people with three different surnames. One day the doorbell rang and the inquisitive letter carrier asked, "Should I be delivering all this mail to your address?"

"It's only temporary, "Edith apologized. "I hope you don't mind."

"It doesn't bother me," he quickly assured her. "But I was worried that there might be some mistake." Actually, Edith was surprised he even noticed the extra names.

She couldn't understand why, but she knew this tall, not exactly handsome, mailman was making excuses the last time he rang her doorbell. Handing her an advertisement he said, "I ran out of these yesterday and I can't remember where I stopped. Did you get one like this?"

Edith looked at him and laughed, "Yes, I did." It was a cold November day so she added, "Is this an excuse to get warm?" He just stood there and smiled at her. Then she remembered a cartoon she had read in the newspaper and asked, "Did you see that comic about the mailman in last night's paper?"

"No," he answered. "I don't read the paper."

"Oh really, I thought everybody did. It doesn't really matter but the cartoon reminded me of you."

"Is that so? I'd like to read it. Have you still got it around?" It was on the coffee table so she picked it up and handed it to him.

The cartoon depicted a mailman who is delighted when he delivers good news, miserable when he delivers bad news and then decides he is getting too emotionally involved with his job. Edith expected her mailman to get a kick out this, but he handed the paper back to her and said, "I don't get it." At first she thought he was teasing her, but then he added seriously, "Would you mind explaining it to me?" This seemed a little strange, but she patiently described her interpretation of the cartoon.

"I don't catch on to things very easily," he apologized. "But now I see what you mean." He looked down at her and smiled. She wasn't sure what amused him but she was getting anxious for him to leave so she could close the door. Her bare feet were getting cold and the pale blue jogging suit wasn't very warm. He noticed her shiver, but instead of leaving, he reached over and closed the door.

"I should have shut the door sooner. You're getting cold." Why didn't he leave? Standing there beside this tall uniformed man, she suddenly felt like a little girl. Her habit of going barefooted made her feel even more childish. But there was no cause for alarm. After all she was a little old lady of fifty-seven and he was just a pesky young mailman.

I almost forgot to give you your mail," he said, as he reached into his bag and pulled out her letters.

"Oh thank you. Does everyone get such personal service?" Edith teased.

He laughed, then commented, "I see you got another big envelope from that writing school. Are you actually taking a writing course?"

"Yes. Writing is one of my hobbies."

"That's interesting." He didn't say, "at your age," but Edith was sure he was thinking it. "What do you write about?"

"Oh, I dabble with fiction. Mostly short stories."

"I'd love to read one."

"You would?" Edith was flattered. Not even her best friends wanted to read her work and this young man seemed so sincere. Then Edith was puzzled. When he had read the

84

cartoon, he didn't seem very interested in reading. So she said, "I have an extra copy of my latest. You can take it with you and be on your way. I can make another copy on the computer if I need it."

He dropped his mailbag on the floor and replied, "I may as well read it here."

"Don't you have to finish your mail route? It will take you at least twenty minutes to read it."

"It's O.K I'm ahead of schedule anyway." Edith thought mail carriers were always in a hurry, but she left the room to get the manuscript. When she returned she was surprised to find that he had kicked off his boots, removed his jacket and was comfortably seated in a big chair. She thought that this was a little brazen and nervously handed him her story.

For a few minutes Edith wondered what to do while he read the story. To be polite she asked him if he would like a cup of coffee. His strange eyes made her feel very uncomfortable. He seemed to see her only from the waist down and she felt self conscious in her snug fitting jogging suit and bare feet. She expected him to refuse the coffee, but instead he flashed his wide smile and answered, "Coffee would be great."

His eyes followed her as she escaped into the kitchen. She felt like changing into something less revealing, so to cover her bare feet she shoved them into her slippers that were under the table. Then she scolded herself, "Don't be ridiculous. Are you stupid enough to think a young man like this would be interested in an old woman's body? He's just being nice, that's all." Now that she set herself straight Edith was able to make the coffee.

Feeling a little guilty for thinking such terrible things about him, she even added a muffin with the coffee and sat the snack or the table in front of him. "I'll leave you to your misery," she told him cheerfully. "My computer is on so I'll continue typing. Just give me a shout when you're finished."

The privacy of her office was a relief. Edith settled down to her keyboard and time passed quickly. She expected her friendly critic to call out a polite, "Thank you, your story is great," and leave.

To her amazement and alarm, she glanced up from her work and saw him standing in the open doorway. She wondered why he looked so different. Then realized she had never seen him without his hat and now dark hair fell onto his forehead, changing his whole appearance. What frightened her the most, was the amusement in his wide-open, glossy eyes.

"That's a great story," he praised. He even sounded sincere.

Before Edith could get up to graciously bid him farewell, he came over and stood behind her. She sat very still as he began to softly read words from the monitor. Then he asked, "Is this how you write your stories? I have never seen anyone type with a computer before. How do you get it onto paper?"

He really bugged her standing behind her. She could feel him breathing on her hair. She tried to calm down so she could demonstrate how the word processor and the printer worked.

"Fascinating," he commented. But she noticed he was looking at her software instead of the computer hardware. She hurried out of the office, expecting him to follow her back to the front door. He stopped her outside the office door with a restraining hand on her shoulder. Looking down at her with his ear to ear grin, he asked, "Can I see the rest of your house? It sure looks at lot bigger from the inside." He was looking down the hallway towards the bedrooms.

Now Edith was truly alarmed. She tried to put him off. "There's… there's only a bathroom and two bedrooms, nothing special. And I'm not a very good housekeeper."

"Oh, don't worry about that. I don't keep things very tidy either." He grabbed her hand and led her down the hall.

In that few seconds Edith's whole life passed before her eyes. She was terrified. Physically, she was no match for this giant. She had never attracted the opposite sex and couldn't believe this was happening to her. "Maybe I'm jumping to conclusions," she told herself. But the comfort of that thought didn't last long.

The pressure of his hand was demanding. Leading her into the spare bedroom, he said, "I love this room. It looks so comfy. Let's sit down."

Edith was doomed. If she fought she was sure he would strangle her. Even if he guessed that she was afraid she knew her life would be in danger. Had he already detected her terror? Her only hope was to outwit him. So Edith looked up at him and forced a smile.

They were sitting on the bed and to her surprise he released her hand. Not looking directly at her, he said, "That shy girl in your story is you, isn't it?" She didn't trust her voice, so she just nodded and he went on. "I'm shy like that too." Edith was finding that a little hard to believe. "My brother tells me I'm no good," he continued. "He says I'm too soft because I don't stick up for myself. I thought of writing too, but my sister told me I was crazy. She says I would have known long ago if I had any talent for writing."

"Oh no!" she interjected. "That's not true. You're never too old to follow a dream. Don't let anyone put you down." What a stupid thing to say! But, for a moment Edith had felt sorry for him.

"You really believe that, don't you?" Afraid to say any more, she just nodded. Now that he was talking the danger did not seem so close. Then she reminded herself that they were still sitting on a bed. "Should I try to escape?" she wondered. "No, that would make him angry and he could easily overtake me." So she decided to try sweetness again.

"I'll bet you don't know how late it is?" she said, hoping to break this spell. He looked down at her tight jogging pants again. Her fear returned.

"I've got lots of time," he replied. "Besides I like talking to you." Was that all he wanted to do? Just talk! Then why did he lead her into this bedroom?

She had to keep him talking, so she responded with a simple, "Oh."

"Usually it's hard for me to talk to people, especially women."

"Maybe you're not looking for them in the right place."

His eyelids closed over his large eyes as he looked down at his fidgeting hands. "You could be right," he confessed. "Actually I'm very lonesome. When I read your story I realized we are the same. You're unhappy too, aren't you?"

Edith's fear had faded as they talked, but now she didn't like the way this conversation was going. So she got up and said, "I have to get back to my typing and I'm sure you have to finish your route."

He immediately pulled her back onto the bed and mumbled, "Just as I thought. You're afraid to talk about yourself. I know how you feel." The arm around her shoulders smothered her.

Terrified. Her thoughts raced. No one to help. Can't run. Must keep him talking. Can't speak. Smile. I can't. Yes, you can. Smile! Smile! Smile!

Edith smiled and he smiled back. Did he hear the thumping of her heart? He was talking. What was he saying? "You make me feel so comfortable. It's nice to talk to someone who actually likes me. You just smile and listen." Actually she couldn't speak and it was a forced smile that was pasted on her face.

Suddenly he put his hand on her thigh. Her smile froze. Her voice froze. Her whole body froze. He did not notice her icy condition but went on excitedly, "At one time I was very shy. But now I'm a little wild and I think you are too. Aren't you?" She couldn't answer. "Aren't you?" he repeated.

Edith fought to control herself. "I can't speak. You must. I can't. Smile. Don't make him angry. What should I do? Do something. Say something. Dear God, give me strength."

With the smile stuck to her face, she gently lifted his large red hand from her thigh. She rose from the bed. Her legs wobbled. Words must have come from above. She was surprised she could speak. She was even more surprised at what she said. "I know you didn't mean any harm. And I'm sorry if I led you on. But, I'll let you guess how I have stayed happily married for over thirty-eight years."

She didn't move. He didn't move. Time didn't move. She was at his mercy. He got up. He looked down at her. She looked up at him. Smile still glued on. His hand is on her shoulder. He is sad.

Relief. He's sad, not mad. Relief. Relief. Relief.

"I'm sorry." His hand is off her shoulder. He is at the bedroom door. He says, "My God, it's hot in here!" and disappears.

She falls onto the bed. Can't move. Can't think. Stares at the ceiling. Door slams. She lies there. She cries. She cries louder. She bawls.

Edith has a new letter carrier. She is thankful it is a woman.

Lady Valentine

Lady Valentine

Editor's Note

Nineteen sixty-one saw the birth of the seventh child for Alice and Bob McNeish. There would still be two more. They named their seventh child Evelyn Grace Lillian. During a previous pregnancy Alice had become very ill and her friend Evelyn Witmer helped care for her family. The baby was named Evelyn to honour this special friendship. Evelyn Witmer and her husband Ross were appointed as godparents.

In nineteen sixty-three a local radio station was running a contest for Lady Valentine and

Alice was so appreciative of her friend that she entered Mrs. Witmer in the contest. With the entry she submitted a poem.

When Evelyn Witmer realized I was publishing a book of my mom's stories she asked if it would include the poem my mom wrote. I finally agreed to have a look at it. The following is from a scan of the work sent to me by Evelyn Witmer. I blocked out information that would indicate specific addresses or phone numbers as those would no longer be valid and may now belong to others.

A Valentine Ode
To My Dear Friend Evelyn

The dear old Saint of long ago,
Would wish that he had known,
The one I wish to tell about,
Of whom, I write this poem.

Sometime ago when I was ill,
With many things to do,
I had no one to call upon
My friends were very few.

When this dear lady learned about
The trouble I was in,
She came right over to my house
And cared for all my kin.

2.

She washed and ironed and cleaned and canned,
The strawberries were ripe.
She picked and stemmed and froze them all.
To waste, she's not the type.

That was the start of our friendship,
A long and lasting one.
Don't go yet I'll tell you more.
This rhyme has just begun.

The lovely lady is not known
For famous acts or deeds;
But for the little things she does
To help the one who needs.

3

With three children of her own,
She is very busy.
Yet she always takes the time
To help Lil or Lizzy.

The neighbour who lives next to her
Had a brand new baby.
The other children were in the care
Of this charming lady.

When I was in the hospital,
Three times to be exact,
My mother could not visit me.
Evelyn came, in fact.

4

We call her grandma for our kids
Although she is not old.
I named my seventh after her,
She's proud of that, I'm told.

On Sunday morning very early
She helps her man at church.
They organize our Sunday School.
For teachers, we'll not search.

Although she is not president
Of our ladies' group,
She's always there to help us out
When we are in the soup.

5

An evening out with her hubby
Along with Dan and wife
Would give her much to remember
The rest of her sweet life.

Evelyn Witmer is the name
Of this dear friend of mine.
Please help me pay a debt and make
Her Lady Valentine.

Written, with the greatest
sincerity, by
Alice McNeish.

(over)

6.

As you have guessed by now, I am nominating Mrs Evelyn Witmer, ██████ Connaught St., Kitchener as Lady Valentine. Her phone no. is ██████

The preceding fourteen (for the 14th) verses of rhyme do not adequately describe my Lady Valentine. In fact, no words (especially mine) can really show how I feel. However I would like to add that Evelyn is the type of person who is usually taken for granted. She is one who, so quietly and inconspicuously goes about spreading the feeling of love

7

and good-will. I would like to be more specific but I do not wish to embarrass her many friends who listen regularly to C K K W. Although they do not know I have nominated her, they always listen closely for contest winners. I shall close by thanking the judges for their kind consideration of this entry.

Sincerely,

{ My phone no is ██████ Rural party line always busy! }

Mrs Alice McNeish
R.R.2, Kitchener

P. S. The picture on the cover is Evelyn holding her namesake. It was taken last spring when little Evelyn was baptized. Please save this entry because I would like my friend to have it whether she wins or not.

ENDNOTES

These are the works of my mom which I have discovered. If there are others, I am not aware of them. This book is an attempt to render these stories as they were written with only minor changes to correct obvious errors.

The final piece was the earliest work I have of Alice McNeish, and since it was done in her own hand I presented it that way. I only cropped, grey scaled and resized the original to make it fit this book.

The dream of being a writer is one my mother nurtured for a long time. She struggled with it throughout her school days and had to fight to get a high school education. Her parents did not believe that a farm girl needed an education, so they saw no necessity. She completed high school in 1948 and her father's prediction came true. She married and soon started a family. In 1950 their first child was born and that continued until their ninth child was born in 1968.

Her dream reared its head again in 1971, and cried out for recognition in 1986. The stories in this book were written as part of a course she took that year. I've also included a poem she wrote 23 years prior to that.

Seventy years after Alice McNeish put her dream on hold and 32 years after the main body of her work was written, it is now finally published.

Bob and Alice McNeish
Oct 30, 1948

Bob and Alice McNeish
Oct 30, 2016

McNeish Family circa 1986

Published in honour of Alice Sarah (Horsburgh) McNeish who put the needs of others before her own.

She was born in 1929. To this day there is no end to her love which is offered equally to all.

"**Love is love. You cannot love someone more or love someone less**"

Alice McNeish

Preparing this book has been a labour of love. My mother, Alice Sarah McNeish, is the wisest woman I know. Even in recent years when her memory so often fails her, she continues to astound me with her wisdom.

I would also like to recount one story that explains a little of the nature of my mom. In the early 1970's I was walking with a friend when we chanced to meet my mom on the street. We briefly chatted and continued on our way. My friend commented, "Is that your mom? Is she ever nice!"

Before that time I never gave much thought as to the niceness of my mom. She was the only mom I ever knew and I just assumed all moms were like mine. This was my first wakeup call and I began to realize that my mom was special. I soon learned how privileged I was.

Thanks Mom

For being the best mother any
child could ever have.

Proof

Made in the USA
Columbia, SC
20 May 2018